DISCARD

I DARE YOU Not to YAWN

HÉLÈNE BOUDREAU
illustrated by SERGE BLOCH

CANDLEWICK PRESS

First edition 2013

Library of Congress Cataloging-in-Publication Data is available.

Library of Congress Catalog Card Number pending

ISBN 978-0-7636-5070-4

12 13 14 15 16 17 LEO 10 9 8 7 6 5 4 3 2 1

Printed in Heshan, Guangdong, China

This book was typeset in Avenir Medium.
The illustrations were hand-drawn with ink and colored digitally.

Candlewick Press
99 Dover Street
Somerville, Massachusetts 02144

visit us at www.candlewick.com

For Marcelle,
who was the first to dare me not to yawn
H. B.

Yawns are sneaky.
They can creep up on you when you least expect them.

There you are, minding your own business, building the tallest block tower in the history of the universe or dressing up the cat when suddenly . . .

your arms stretch up, your eyes squish tight, your mouth opens wide, your tongue curls back, and— *mmm . . . rrr . . . yawwrrrr*—a yawn pops out.

Next thing you know,
you're being sent upstairs
to get your pajamas on!

Pajamas lead to bedtime stories.

Bedtime stories lead to sleepy-time songs.

And sleepy-time songs lead to good-night hugs and kisses.

Before you know it, you're tucked into bed,
snug as a bug, and wondering . . .

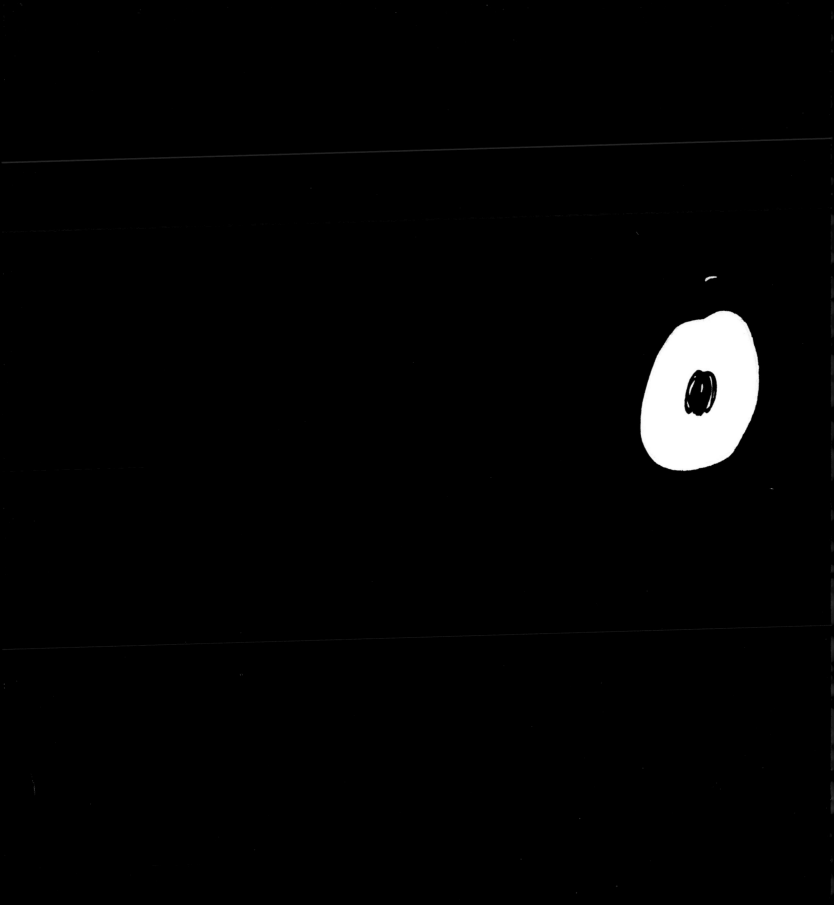

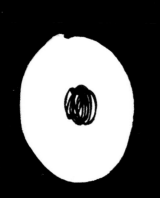

"How did I get here?"

So, if you're not ready to go to bed, follow these tips and DO NOT YAWN!

If someone else yawns, like your baby brother, or your big sister, or the dog—ahhh!—
LOOK AWAY!

Stay away from huggable stuffed animals,
soft cozy pajamas, and your favorite
blankie because—*mm . . . mm . . . mmm*—
those can make you feel snuggly.

Avoid bedtime stories about sleepy baby animals, like tiger cubs arching their backs in one last stretch, their eyes squished tight and their tongues curled back—*rawr . . . rawr . . . rawr*—

or you might start to feel stretchy, too.

Don't sing sleepy-time songs about twinkling stars
or baaing sheep, especially the counting kind—
one sheep, two sheep, *baa . . . baa . . . baaa. . . .*

And WHATEVER YOU DO, don't think of droopy-eyed baby orangutans holding their long arms out for a hug from their mamas . . .

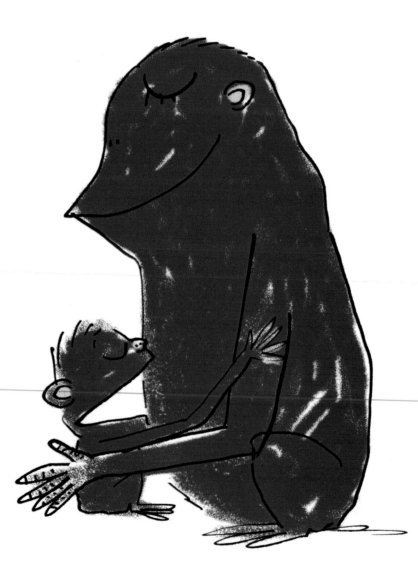

their little mouths forming perfect *o's*— *oh . . . oh . . . oh!*

Uh-oh!

If you try all these things, but a yawn STILL creeps up and grabs a hold of you, QUICK, cover your mouth— *mmpprff!*—to keep it from escaping.

Because if your arms stretch up—
mm . . . mm . . . mmm . . .

your eyes squish tight—
rawr . . . rawr . . . rawrrr . . .

your mouth opens wide—
baa . . . baa . . . baaa . . .

your tongue curls back—
oh . . . oh . . . ohhh . . .

and a yawn pops out—

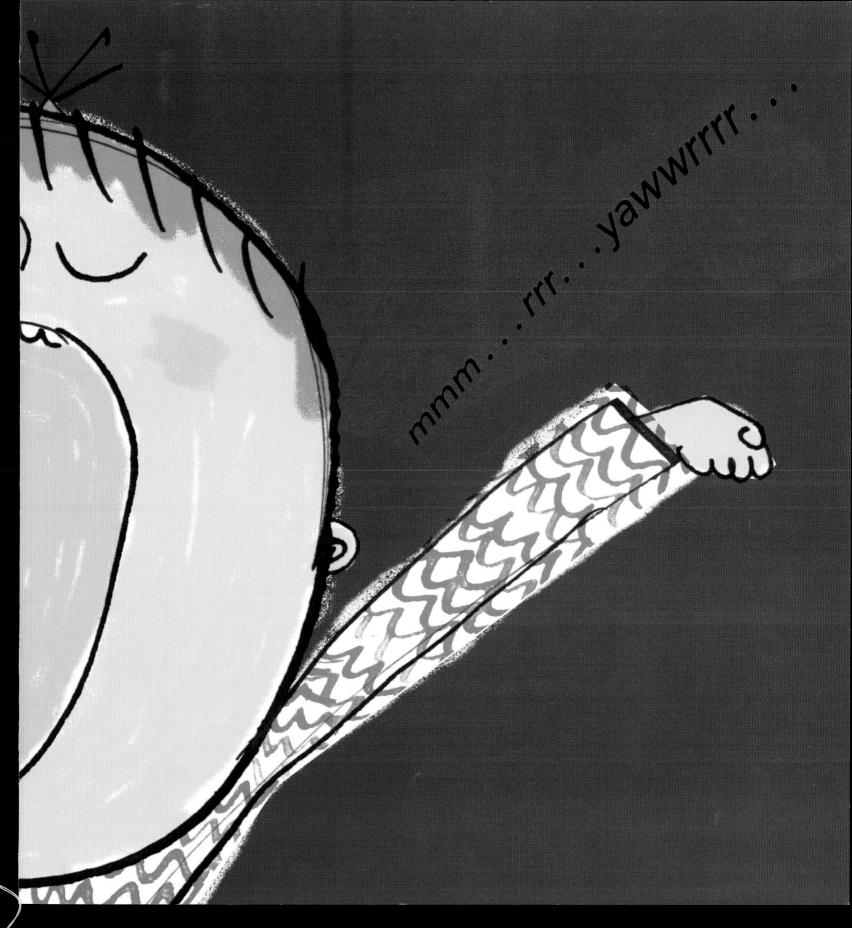

mmm . . . . rrr . . . . yawwrrrr . . .

then off to bed you'll go.

See? I told you.
Yawns are sneaky.